PIPPA MOUSE

SIX READ-ALOUD/READ-ALONE STORIES

by Betty Boegehold

Illustrated by Cyndy Szekeres

Alfred A. Knopf · New York

To Julie and Abby

THIS IS A BORZOI BOOK
PUBLISHED BY ALFRED A. KNOPF, INC.

Copyright © 1973 by BETTY BOEGEHOLD
Illustrations copyright © 1973 by CYNDY SZEKERES PROZZO

Library of Congress Cataloging in Publication Data
Boegehold, Betty Virginia (Doyle) Pippa Mouse.
SUMMARY: Six stories about a little mouse and her animal friends in
the woods.
[1. Short stories] I. Szekeres, Cyndy, illus.
II. Title.
PZ10.3.B637Pi [E] 73-4916
ISBN 0-394-82671-X
ISBN 0-394-92671-4 (lib. bdg.)

Manufactured in the United States of America

The Stories

Her Mouse House

Rain is falling
outside the mouse-hole house.
Pippa is tired of
watching the rain.
"Mother, tell me a story,"
says Pippa.

"Not yet, dear," says Mother.
"I must make the beds."
"I will help you," says Pippa.

Slip-slap. Slip-slap. Slap-slip.
The beds are made.

"Now is it time for a story?"
asks Pippa.
"Not yet, dear," says Mother.
"Now it is time to sweep."
"I will help you," says Pippa.

Sweep. Sweep.
Brush and sweep.
The sweeping is done.
"Now is it story time?" asks Pippa.

"My goodness!" says Mother
"Look at the rain!
It is coming right into
our mouse-hole house."

The rain is coming down fast,
making big puddles in the green grass,
and little puddles
on the floor of the mouse-hole house.

"I will shut the door," says Pippa.
"You know we have no door," says Mother.
"Then I will make a door,"
says Pippa Mouse.

She takes some wood
from the big woodpile
and puts it all around the hole
of the mouse-hole house.

Then she takes more pieces
from the big woodpile
and nails them together.

Hammer! Hammer!
Bang! Bang! Bang!
With her strong white paws
Pippa makes a door—
a good tight door,
with a good tight frame
all around.

9

"There!" says Pippa.
"I made a door!"
"Thank you, Pippa Mouse,"
says Mother.
"Now we *do* have a door,
and we *don't* have puddles.
So now it is time
for a story."

Mother sits in her chair
by the warm red fire.
Pippa sits in her chair
right beside her Mother.

Mother says,
"Once upon a time,
a big brave mouse
found puddles coming
in her mouse-hole house.
She took a hammer
and with Bing, Bang, Bin!
kept all the water
from blowing right in!
Now, who's snug
as a bug in a rug?
Who's the brave dry mouse
in her new-door house?"

"Oh, Mother," says Pippa.
"I know who it is . . .
ME!"

A New Nest

Gray Bird is making a nest in a bush.
Around and around she turns,
making a soft cup of a nest.

"That's a pretty good nest," says Pippa.
"Strong on the outside
and soft on the inside."
"Climb in," says Gray Bird.

Pippa sits down in the nest.
Gray Bird sits down too—
right on top of Pippa.
Under her wings, Pippa is warm—
too warm to breathe.
So out of the nest she climbs.

"A good nest," says Pippa,
"but much too small
for a big mouse and a bird.
Goodbye."

Then Pippa Mouse sees Ripple Squirrel
racing up and down the old oak tree.
Ripple is carrying leaves in her mouth
to make a summer nest
high in the old oak tree.
"Hi, Pippa," says Ripple.
"Come up and rock in my nest with me."

So up the tree goes Pippa,
out on a branch and into Ripple's nest.

Up and down goes the branch.
Up and down goes the next branch.
Up and down, and down and up
go Ripple Squirrel and Pippa.

"I don't feel very well," says Pippa.
"The ground is too far away,
and this nest rocks too much.
Too much rocking for me.
Goodbye," says Pippa.

Down on the ground, Pippa says,
"I will make a nest myself.
Big and soft and round
and down on the ground.
It will be the best nest
in the world!"

Pippa takes leaves, sticks and mud.
She pushes them and mushes them
around and around.
Then she calls, "Look, everyone!
I have made a nest—
the best nest in the world!
I will sleep in my nest tonight
under the moon and the stars."

"I don't see any stars," says Father Mouse,
coming out of the mouse-house.
"And I don't see any moon.
It looks like rain to me."

"No, no, it will not rain," says Pippa.
"Squirrels and birds
are sleeping in their nests.
I will sleep in my nest too."

"Goodnight then, my nestling,"
says Father Mouse.

Darkness fills the sky.
Then Pippa hears a little noise—
plop–drop–plop–drop.
Plop-drop, plop-drop.
First one raindrop,
then another.
Now it is raining hard.

Gray Bird puts her head
under her wing
and keeps on sleeping.
Ripple Squirrel spreads her fluffy tail
like an umbrella
and keeps on sleeping.
But Pippa Mouse does not.
She gets wet.

"Who is that?" asks Father Mouse.
"Who is coming in soft as a leaf?"

"Just Pippa," says Pippa,
hopping into her bed.
"Birds and squirrels
can sleep out in the rain,
but a big wet mouse
wants a cozy bed
in a dry mouse-house."

Noisy Pippa

Pippa Mouse sits on Weber Duck's back.
Weber is taking her for a ride
across the lake.

"Sit still," says Weber Duck.
"You wiggle too much.
You will fall off."

"No," says Pippa. "I won't fall off.
I want to wiggle and dance.
Look at the mouse dancing—
dancing on the duck in the lake."

SPLASH!

"Well, anyhow
I had a good swim," says Pippa.

On the shore, Gray Bird is watching a stone.
Halfway under the stone,
a beetle is watching Gray Bird.

"Hi, Gray Bird," shouts Pippa.
"I've been swimming.
Look at how wet I am!"

"Shh, Pippa," Gray Bird says, "be very quiet.
I am waiting for that beetle to come out."

"I *am* quiet," says Pippa.
"Just listen to how quiet I am!
I do not scream or yell or even talk.
I am as quiet as this beetle."

Pippa tapped the beetle.
With his two feelers,
the beetle tapped Pippa, then went away,
back under the stone.

"Oh Pippa, you've frightened the beetle away.
Now you go away too, Pippa Mouse,"
says Gray Bird.
"I don't want to stay here anyhow,"
says Pippa.
"I want to make noise."

Pippa finds a clump of mushrooms.
"Here are my bongo drums," says Pippa.
"Listen to me playing
on my red bongo drums.
Booma, booma, boom!"

"Quiet down there," calls Ripple Squirrel,
high in the old oak tree.
"I am trying to take a nap.
Be quiet, Pippa Mouse."

"I do not want to be quiet,
and I will not be quiet,
and I *can't* be quiet!"
says Pippa Mouse.
"I will play on my red bongo drums.
I will make all the noise I want to.
Booma, booma, boom!"

"Yes, keep on making noise,"
softly calls Red Fox.
"Please make lots of noise,
so I can find you, Pippa Mouse."

Now everything is quiet—
very, very quiet.
Where is noisy Pippa Mouse?
Hiding under a log, she is
quiet as a blink,
quiet as a wink,
quiet as a mouse.

A Good Game

"Come and play with me," says Pippa Mouse.
"Not now," says Ripple Squirrel.
"I must work today.
I must gather nuts."

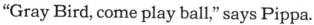

"Gray Bird, come play ball," says Pippa.
"Not now," says Gray Bird,
"I must work today.
I have to hunt for seeds."

"Weber Duck, you play ball with me,"
calls Pippa.
"No, no! I am working now," says Weber.
"I am diving deep for weeds."

"Then I'll play ball anyhow," says Pippa.
"I'll play by myself."

She finds a pebble and a stick.
She bats the pebble with the stick.
She kicks the pebble here and there,
until the pebble gets lost in the grass.
Then Pippa says,
"I must work today, too.
I can't play all day
with sticks and pebbles.
I'm a very busy mouse."

She sweeps off a big flat rock.
She puts small stone stools around it.
She puts four flower cups on the big rock,
and four flat leaves for plates.
Then she gets something else—
something good to eat
from her mouse-hole house.

"Ripple and Gray Bird
and Weber Duck," calls Pippa,
"now you can stop work.
Now it is time to play a game with me."

"I am too busy," says Ripple.
"I am too busy," says Gray Bird.
And Weber Duck says, "I am too busy
and too tired—
too tired to play, Pippa Mouse."

"You will not be too tired for this game,"
says Pippa.
"For this game is called
Everybody-Sit-Down-And-Eat!"

"I am not too busy at all," says Gray Bird,
flying to the big flat stone.
"I am not too tired after all," says Weber,
waddling over on his flat yellow feet.
"I will play this game," says Ripple Squirrel.
"I will play this game with you right now!"

"It is a good game," says Pippa,
"because nobody loses,
everybody wins!"

Ice Mice

Pippa looks at the puddle.
It is shiny and still.
Pippa jumps on the puddle,
and crinkles it all to bits.
"Hurray! It's ice!" yells Pippa.
"Let's go skating, Weber Duck."

"Don't be silly," says Weber.
"My webbed feet are for swimming,
not for skating."

"How about you, Gray Bird?"
calls Pippa.
"Will you go skating with me?"

"Not I," says Gray Bird.
"My feet are too curly for skating."

Then Ripple Squirrel says,
"I'll come with you, Pippa.
If you will try, I will try."

Down on the gray lake ice,
Ripple and Pippa
go sliding.
First on four feet,
then on two feet,
then—BUMP—on no feet!

"If at first you don't succeed,"
says Pippa, "try, try again.
Let's find some skates."

Scribble, scrabble! Scratch and hunt.
They find eight smooth stones—
one for each of their eight little paws.
They hold the stones in their paws
and push off over the ice.

"Look at my skates!" calls Pippa.
"I have four skates,
and I am skating!"

Then out go Pippa's feet
and down goes Pippa.
And down goes Ripple Squirrel
right on top of Pippa!

"I have four feet and
they go four ways," says Pippa.
"So do I," says Ripple.
"Let's try again."

Scribble, scrabble. Scratch and hunt.
They find some peelings of bark
from the big white birch tree.

"We do not have ice skates," says Pippa.
"We have iceboats instead.
We will slide across the ice
on our birchbark sleds."

Ripple Squirrel sits on her sled
and holds up her tail for a sail.
Pippa Mouse sits
on her birchbark sled
and holds up a dry birch leaf
fastened to the mast of her tail.

An icy wind begins to blow
across the lake,
pushing Ripple and Pippa
over the dark lake ice.
"Hurray!" calls Pippa.
"Here we go on our iceboats
over the icy sea."

"I will call my iceboat *Sailor Squirrel*,"
says Ripple,
blowing along like a leaf.

"And I will call my boat *Ice Mice*,"
says Pippa,
sailing along beside her.
"*Ice Mouse*, you mean," says Ripple.
"No," says Pippa.
"For I will get my father and my mother
and give them a ride this very afternoon!"

"Hurray, sing hurray,
for the three brave mice!
Who'll sail far away
on the dark gray ice?
Who'll sail the *Ice Mice*
so far out to sea?
Mother, Father and Captain—
and the Captain is ME!"

Not-Even, A Mouse

Christmas time is here.
Pippa Mouse wants
to hang up a Christmas stocking.

"But we don't have any stockings,"
says Mother.
"Then I will hang up something else,"
says Pippa.
"What can I hang up?"

47

Pippa looks and looks.
Mother looks too.

"There is nothing else to hang up,"
says Mother.
"Yes there is," says Pippa.
"I will hang up my swimming cap.
It is big and round.
It will hold more than a stocking—
much, much more."

49

"That looks very funny," says Mother.
"No, that looks very good," says Pippa.
"Now tell me the story of Not-Even."
"Who is Not-Even?" asks Mother.
"You know," says Pippa.
"Stop fooling me."

50

Mother says,
"'Twas the night before Christmas
And all through the house,
Not a creature was stirring,
Not-Even, a mouse ... !

"Now be like Not-Even,
and go to sleep,
for tomorrow is Christmas Day,"
says Mother.

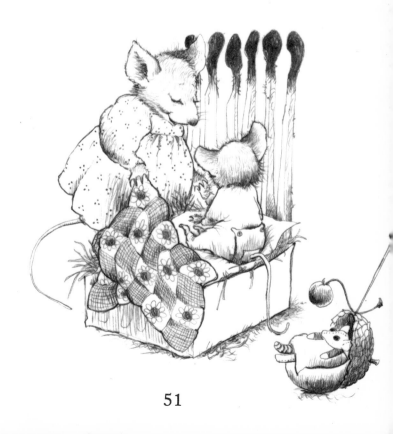

The next morning, someone says,
"Merry Christmas, Pippa."
The someone is Father.

"Merry Christmas," calls Someone Else.
The Someone Elses are Mother,
Ripple Squirrel, Gray Bird and Weber Duck.

"Merry Christmas, everyone," says Pippa.

Here is Pippa's Christmas tree.

Here is Pippa's swimming cap,
and here are some things in it—
many, many things.

Pippa puts on her swimming cap,
and plays with her Christmas things.

Then Pippa pulls some other things
out from behind her bed.

Here is something for Mother and Father.

Here is something for Ripple Squirrel,

for Gray Bird and Weber Duck, too.
"Hurray for Christmas," says Pippa.

Everyone plays a game,
everyone sings songs,
everyone sits down for Mother's dinner.

Then Pippa Mouse is sleepy.
"I would like Christmas
to last forever," says Pippa.

"What?" asks Father Mouse.
"And never have time to swim?
Or roll nuts?
Or run and play?
Or even try to fly?"

"Well," says Pippa,
"I want those times too.
But not right now.
Right now,
I don't want anything at all."

"Nothing at all, my Pippa?"
asks Mother.

"Yes, one thing," says Pippa.

"Right now, I want to go to sleep."

Betty Boegehold has been active in elementary education for many years. She is currently a writer, editor, and graduate instructor at New York's Bank Street College of Education—a specialist in beginning-reader materials.

Cyndy Szekeres is well-known for her irresistible animal characters. Some of her books have been Junior Literary Guild Selections, and she received an **AIGA** award for *Moon Mouse,* published by Random House. She is the creator of the popular *Cyndy's Animal Calendars* and *Cyndy's Workbook Diary.*

Chucky Aeigrut
Room 7ms Hi
gbi